The
BOOK That ATE
My
BROTHER

BY MICHAEL DAHL

Illustrated by
Bradford Kendall

STONE ARCH BOOKS
a capstone imprint

ZONE BOOKS ARE PUBLISHED BY
STONE ARCH BOOKS
A CAPSTONE IMPRINT
151 GOOD COUNSEL DRIVE, P.O. BOX 669
MANKATO, MINNESOTA 56002
WWW.CAPSTONEPUB.COM

LIBRARY OF CONGRESS CATALOGING-IN-PUBLICATION DATA
DAHL, MICHAEL.
  THE BOOK THAT ATE MY BROTHER / WRITTEN BY MICHAEL DAHL ;
ILLUSTRATED BY BRADFORD KENDALL.
      P. CM. -- (RETURN TO THE LIBRARY OF DOOM)
  ISBN 978-1-4342-2144-5 (LIBRARY BINDING)
 (1. BROTHERS--FICTION. 2. BOOKS AND READING--FICTION. 3.
HORROR STORIES.) I. KENDALL, BRADFORD, ILL. II. TITLE.
  PZ7.D15134BOL 2010
  (FIC)--DC22   2010004032

ART DIRECTOR: KAY FRASER
GRAPHIC DESIGNER: HILARY WACHOLZ
PRODUCTION SPECIALIST: MICHELLE BIEDSCHEID

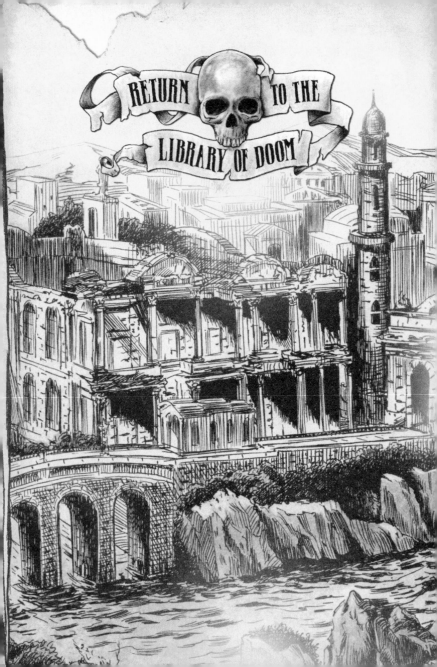

RETURN TO THE
LIBRARY OF DOOM

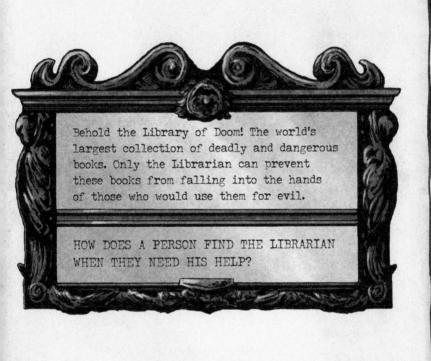

Behold the Library of Doom! The world's largest collection of deadly and dangerous books. Only the Librarian can prevent these books from falling into the hands of those who would use them for evil.

HOW DOES A PERSON FIND THE LIBRARIAN WHEN THEY NEED HIS HELP?

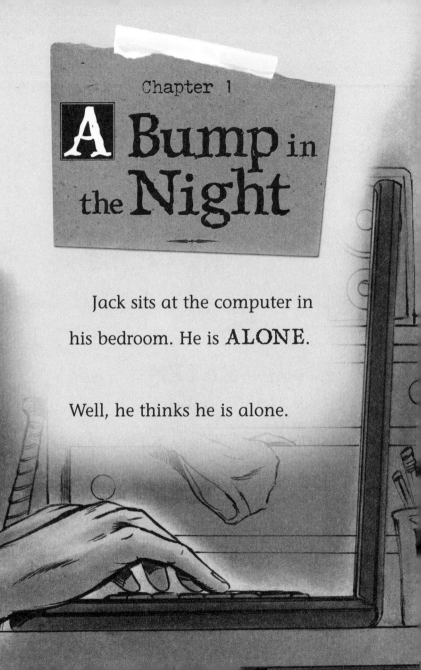

Chapter 1
A Bump in the Night

Jack sits at the computer in his bedroom. He is **ALONE**.

Well, he thinks he is alone.

Dear <u>*Librarian*</u>*,* he types.

I need your help. My brother Tyler needs your help.

He has been **EATEN** *by a book.*

I found a website called The Library of Doom, Jack types.

I don't know if you'll read this or not. But if you do, you are the ONLY *person who can help us.*

I have heard that you destroy books that are evil. Well, this book is definitely evil!

Jack hears a **noise** behind him.

He quickly **TURNS** around.

He walks over to the bedroom door
and makes sure it is LOCKED.

He hears a bump and rustling **SOUNDS** in the hall outside.

Jack returns to his computer. *You have to help me*, he types. *Before the book eats me next.*

Jack hears another **BUMP** outside the door. Then another.

The bumps are growing louder. Jack begins to type <u>faster</u>.

Chapter 2

The Hungry Book

It all started when Tyler found the book in the **DOGHOUSE**, Jack types.

Tyler was looking for our dog, Buck.

?

Buck had been **MISSING** *all day.*

?   ?

When Tyler looked in Buck's doghouse, he saw a book inside.

The book was very **old** *and very big.*

13

Tyler had **TROUBLE** reading the cover.

He thought it was an adventure book.

CHEWS
YOUR OWN
ADVENTURE

WRITTEN BY
DR. VORACIOUS TOME

Tyler brought the book inside. He took it up to his room to check it out.

He had **FORGOTTEN** *all about Buck.*

Tyler tried to open the book, but couldn't.

He thought the book growled *at him. So he threw it in the closet and shut the door.*

That **night**, *Tyler heard a noise from his closet. Something was bumping in there.*

He came and told me about it, types Jack. *But I didn't* **believe** *him. I thought he was making it all up.*

I told Tyler to go back to his room.

So he did. That was the **LAST** *time I saw him.*

My parents think that Tyler *ran* away.

But I know what really happened.

That book **ATE** him.

I know, because I saw its mouth.

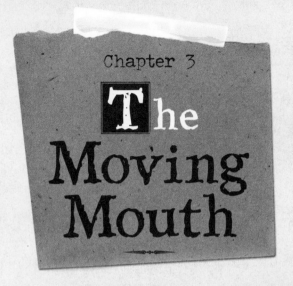

Chapter 3

The Moving Mouth

We looked for **TYLER** *the next day,*
Jack types.

I looked in his closet. I saw an <u>OLD</u>
*book in there. I figured it must have been
the book he talked about.*

I picked it up and opened it.

It was weird. On the first page was a picture of a big **MOUTH**.

I was going to turn the page, but then the mouth moved.

It **MOVED** its lips toward my hand.

I think I even saw part of a **TOOTH**.

I threw the book into the closet. It hit the floor.

Then I saw the cover flip open.

The mouth moved like it was chewing something.

That's when I heard it.

The **VOICE**.

It came from far away, and sounded just like Tyler yelling.

"Jack," said the voice. "Save me!"

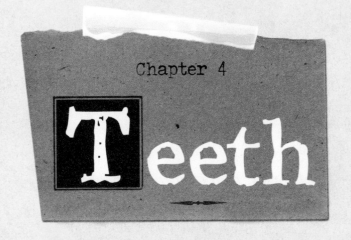

Chapter 4

Teeth

"Tyler!" I yelled. "Where are you?"

"I'm inside," he called. "INSIDE
the book! Jack, you have to help me!"

I took a step toward the book. It
growled. *Then it jumped at me!*

You should have seen the teeth on
that thing.

I RAN out of Tyler's room and came in here.

That's when I thought of you, types Jack.

I read somewhere that you help people when they have **TROUBLE** *with books.*

Can you help us?

The door to Jack's bedroom **crashes** open. The book is there. Its covers open and shut angrily.

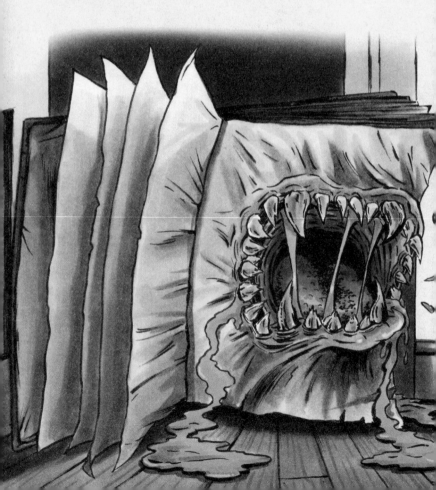

Drool **OOZES** from several of the pages.

"Get away!" yells Jack.

Jack **JUMPS** up on his bed.

He hopes the book will not be able
to reach him up there.

Then the book opens its covers.

The mouth on the front page opens
WIDE.

It keeps opening, wider and wider.

The mouth seems to fill the bedroom.

gggggrrrrrr

There is a **GROWL** and a scream.

Seconds later, Jack disappears.

Only his **SHOES** are left behind,

sitting on the bedroom floor.

Chapter 5

Volume 8

In a nearby town, a young girl
named Iris **REACHES** for a book.

She is at an outdoor library sale.

Iris pulls the BOOK out of a box.

"Look, Mom," she says. "This is the one I was looking for."

Iris reads the cover. "Harry Potter, Volume ATE."

"That's silly," says Iris's mother. "They made a **mistake**. It should say Volume Eight."

"I don't care," says Iris. "I **STILL**

want to get it."

So Iris buys the book.

That afternoon she sits in her room
and begins to **READ**.

The 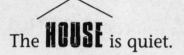**HOUSE** is quiet.

Her parents are next door talking to the neighbors.

Iris opens the book and sees a **picture** on the first page.

It is a picture of a mouth.

Iris hears a **GROWL**.

She thinks it is coming from the book.

She **JUMPS** up from her chair and puts the book on a table.

Suddenly, her younger brother runs into the room. "What's that **noise**?" he asks.

"Don't, Barry," says Iris. "Get away!"

Then Barry sees the <u>book</u> on the table.

The book flips open its cover. The mouth stretches wide.

Iris **screams**. "Barry!"

"Iris!" yells the boy.

The book's mouth seems to fill the
room.

Iris closes her eyes.

Seconds later, her brother is **GONE**.

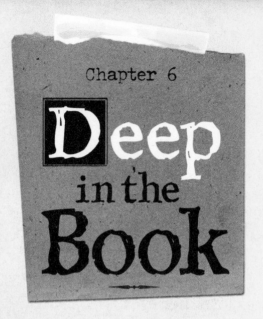

Chapter 6

Deep in the Book

Jack is inside a dark, **SLIMY** tunnel.

The curving walls of the tunnel glow.
Jack can see that the tunnel stretches on
and on.

"Tyler! Where are you?" he yells.

Jack sees a shadow in the tunnel.
As he gets closer, he sees a young boy.
It is not his brother.

"Where did you come from?" asks
Jack.

The boy shakes his head. "I
want my sister," he cries.

"Jack!" comes Tyler's voice. "Help me!"

Jack **CRAWLS** quickly down the slippery tunnel.

The young boy, Barry, follows him.

Jack sees an opening up ahead.

He sees two hands holding on to
the **EDGE** of the tunnel.

"Jack!" yells Tyler.

Jack's **BROTHER** is hanging from
the edge of the tunnel.

Below Tyler's dangling feet is a huge cavern filled with liquid.

The liquid **BUBBLES** and gurgles.

"Pull me up!" shouts Tyler.

Jack and Barry reach toward Tyler. But their hands are **SLIPPERY** from the tunnel.

"I can't hold on!" says Tyler.

Suddenly, a woman appears in the tunnel.

She reaches out a STRONG arm and pulls Tyler to safety.

Then she turns to Jack. "I got your letter," she says.

"Are you the Librarian?" asks Jack.

She shakes her head. "They call me the Specialist," she says. "I help the Librarian now and then."

"You'll see him **soon**," she adds. "But first, let me take care of this."

The Specialist pulls a book out
of her vest. She **HURLS** it into the
bubbling liquid.

"Take a deep breath," says the
Specialist. "And hold on tight!"

The boys grip her hands.

The tunnel begins to **shake** and
thrash.

The liquid **EXPLODES**.

A wall of bubbling goo shoots into the tunnel.

The goo **CRASHES** into the Specialist and the boys.

It forces them back through the tunnel.

Jack feels like toothpaste being SQUEEZED through a tube.

Then he hears a girl scream.

Jack looks up and sees that they are all standing in a strange bedroom.

Barry RUNS toward his sister, Iris.

"What kind of book did you use?"
says a DEEP voice.

A man stands on the other side of
the room.

He is tall and wears DARK glasses
and a long coat.

The man is the Librarian.

The Specialist smiles. "Advanced **ROCKET** science," she replies.

He nods at the Specialist. "Good thinking," he says. "That book is hard to digest."

"This is Jack," says the Specialist. "He's the one who **WROTE** to you."

"Thanks, Jack," says the Librarian.

"We have been hunting that **EVIL** book for months," the Librarian says. "Each mouth hid behind a different cover."

"Are there other mouths?" asks Jack.

"**Five** more," replies the Specialist.

"We need to find the **AUTHOR**," says the Librarian. "Before he writes another book."

"I want to go home," says Tyler. "I need a bath after all that."

The **SPECIALIST** hands Iris a book.

"I think this is the book you were really looking for," she says.

The girl's eyes **LIGHT** up. "Thank you," says Iris.

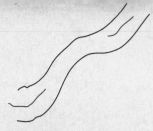

A wind suddenly **BLOWS** through the bedroom.

The two strangers and the older boys are gone.

Iris and Barry look out the window.

They see four shadows flying through the evening **SKY**.

Author

Michael Dahl is the author of more than 200 books for children and young adults. He has won the AEP Distinguished Achievement Award three times for his nonfiction. His Finnegan Zwake mystery series was shortlisted twice by the Anthony and Agatha awards. He has also written the Library of Doom series. He is a featured speaker at conferences around the country on graphic novels and high-interest books for boys.

Illustrator

Bradford Kendall has enjoyed drawing for as long as he can remember. As a boy, he loved to read comic books and watch old monster movies. He graduated from Rhode Island School of Design with a BFA in Illustration. He has owned his own commercial art business since 1983, and lives in Providence, Rhode Island, with his wife, Leigh, and their two children Lily and Stephen. They also have a cat named Hansel and a dog named Gretel.

Glossary

advanced (ad-VANSD)—not easy, high-level

adventure (ad-VEN-chur)—exciting, action-packed

cavern (KAV-ern)—a large cave

digest (dye-JEST)—to understand, or to break down as food

disappears (diss-uh-PIHRZ)—goes out of sight

explodes (ek-SPLODEZ)—blows apart with a loud bang and great force

rustling (RUHSS-uhl-ing)—making a soft, crackling sound

slippery (SLIP-ur-ee)—smooth, oily, wet, hard to grip onto

thrash (THRASH)—to move wildly or violently

tunnel (TUHN-uhl)—a passage built beneath the ground or water

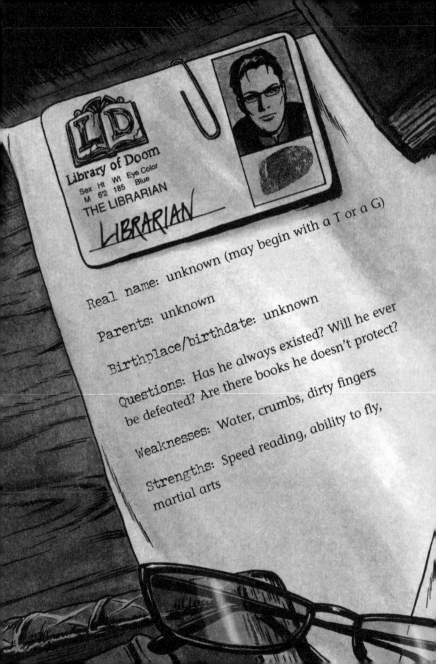

Library of Doom

Sex	Ht	Wt	Eye Color
M	6'2	185	Blue

THE LIBRARIAN

LIBRARIAN

Real name: unknown (may begin with a T or a G)

Parents: unknown

Birthplace/birthdate: unknown

Questions: Has he always existed? Will he ever be defeated? Are there books he doesn't protect?

Weaknesses: Water, crumbs, dirty fingers

Strengths: Speed reading, ability to fly, martial arts

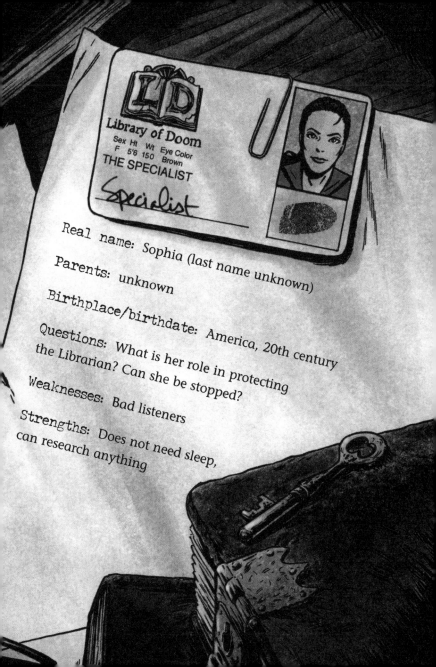

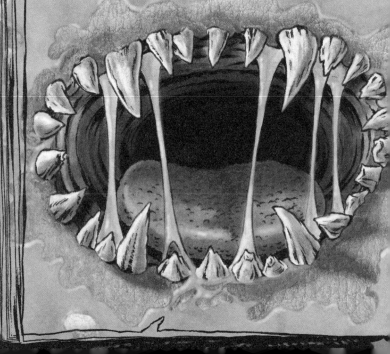

Voracious Tome wants nothing more than to devour readers. He traps them with enchanting rare books — books that they have always wanted to read. Then, when they least expect it, the children are swallowed whole by the books.

Eight mouths have been discovered by the Librarian and his associate, the Specialist. Three have been closed forever — two recently, and one decades ago. But Voracious Tome remains at large, and the five mouths that still exist are open.

The mouths could be in any book. Readers are encouraged to be very careful.

Discussion Questions

1. Why were the books **EATING** children?

2. What did you think about the title of this book? Does it match what you felt when you read the **STORY?**

3. Who is the Librarian? Who is the Specialist?

Writing Prompts

1. Look at the **TITLES** of books in this story. Make a list of books that you would like to read. They can be real books, or you can create your own titles.

2. Imagine that you were eaten by a book. What does it look like inside? What does it **smell** like? What sounds can you hear? What does it feel like? Describe the experience.

3. Write your own **LETTER** to the Librarian.